**To the memory of Tibor Gergely,
Gustaf Tenggren and Garth Williams**

A Night-Light for Bunny

Copyright © 2004 by Geoffrey Hayes

Manufactured in China by South China Printing Company Ltd.

All rights reserved.

www.harperchildrens.com

Library of Congress Cataloging-in-Publication Data is available.

Typography by Fumi Kosaka and Jeanne L. Hogle

1 2 3 4 5 6 7 8 9 10

❖

First Edition

A Night-Light for Bunny

by Geoffrey Hayes

HarperCollins Publishers

"Papa," said Bunny, "I can't sleep. There's too much **dark** at night."

Papa Bunny picked up his bunny child and kissed her square on the nose.

"You need a night-light," he said.

The moon was sailing the sky in her gown of clouds.

"Maybe the moon can be your night-light," said Papa.

But Bunny said, "NO! The moon is too **bright** to be my night-light."

Stars were twinkling in the deep, black sky.

"Pretty as your twinkling eyes," said Papa.
"Maybe the stars can be your night-light."

Bunny said, "No! The stars are too **twinkly** to be a good light for me."

They found fireflies dancing over the
lettuce field, busy being busy.

"Fireflies?" asked Papa.
"Too **busy**," said Bunny.

Bunny found a little glowworm. But it could not be Bunny's night-light. It was already its own night-light.

Papa found another light on a boat on the water.

He sang:

> The ferryman hums in the quiet night,
> safe on his boat
> in his lantern's light.

Bunny said, "That light is almost too **small** for me to see."

"True," said Papa. "Still, it's nice to know it's there."

House lights, porch lights, streetlights—all kinds of lights—glowed in the warm night on the rabbit hill.

"Look, Bunny," said Papa, "the night is *filled* with light!"

Bunny sighed. "I know. But we still haven't found a light for me."

"I don't suppose you'd consider a street-light?" Papa asked.

Bunny stomped her little foot. "Papa, be serious! That light is too **tall** to fit in my room!"

Papa scratched his ears. "Oh, you want a light for your *room*! Well, of course you do. I must have dust bunnies on the brain! Let's go ask Mama."

So Papa and Bunny went back home to their cozy rabbit burrow and asked Mama if she knew of a light for Bunny.

"Oh, that's easy," said Mama. "Grandma gave me a light when I was a little girl, and I believe I know just where it is."

Papa and Bunny followed Mama . . .

to the back of the house, down a wooden
stair.

And close among the beet roots in the warm
earth was a little door.

Inside the door was a little room.
Inside the room was a little box,
And inside the box was . . .
a little lamp.
It wasn't too busy, it wasn't too small,
it wasn't too twinkly,
too bright or too tall.
And . . .

it made wonderful shadows of ships on the wall!

"Oh, Mama, Papa! Thank you!" cried Bunny. "This one is **perfect**!"

The little boat rocks on the water,
Shadow ships sail through the air,
And bunnies can sleep
Through the darkening deep
Of the night without a care;
For there's always a light somewhere.
There's always a light somewhere.

Good night.